# SHINE

## Donnelle McGee

SiblingRivalryPress

Alexander, Arkansas
www.SiblingRivalryPress.com

Shine

Cover photograph by Catskills Photography. Used by permission.

Author photo by Carmen Pegan. Used by permission.

Cover design by Mona Z. Kraculdy.

Sibling Rivalry Press, LLC
13913 Magnolia Glen Drive
Alexander, AR 72002
info@siblingrivalrypress.com
www.siblingrivalrypress.com

ISBN: 978-1-937420-19-2
Library of Congress Control No.: 2012939342
First Sibling Rivalry Press Print Edition, August 2012

SHINE ON YOU CRAZY DIAMOND

— Pink Floyd

for my mother and brother


the healing is in the falling

# I

When I met Shelly I figured I would give up renting my body to the men who rolled up and down Drexel Street, tongues damn near hanging out their windows. But the money is too damn good. Plus I got my sweet spot on Drexel. Got my regulars too.

I ain't gay though.

## II

What are you going to do now? Tell me that Bray. Can you tell me that, can you?

# III

My pops said I damn near flew out of momma's middle. Boy wasn't no stoppin' you. Your momma went to the hospital at 7:19 in the morning. Shit, you was here at 8. And you still in a hurry.

Slow your little ass down.

# IV

I can make about 4 hundy a night. I cap my shit off too. When I'm walking the street I give myself a 3 hour limit. 7-10. Catch them fellas coming from the office. Ain't many of us out here. So the comp. ain't that bad. Shelly don't know how I make all my money. Since we started dating I get out to Drexel 3 sometimes 4 nights out of the week.

I wonder how I ended up doin' some shit like this.

I graduated from Vernon High.

I ain't dumb.

I even enrolled at Salem for a quarter but I couldn't afford books. Some dude in the counseling office told me to apply for financial aid and be patient. Don't worry; you'll get your books soon. I was like naw. I can't be going to class with no books and shit. Be all lost in class. I dropped my classes. Try Salem when I get some more funds.

# V

Shelly. Where you at?

# VI

Bray?

# VII

Drexel, at least the trick turning part of it, runs along the south side of Jillings. It's about a mile or so stretch. 6 motels scattered along its banks. Let's see. You got the Bluethroat Inn, The Drifter, Cloud Nine, Smoke House Roadside Inn, Bennys, and my favorite, the spot where I make my money at, Motel 99. Russell is the manager of the place. He rents me a room by the hour. 12 dollars. I walk the sidewalk and bring my men back to the little room. Most of these dudes just want to release the tension of the day. I lay across the bed for 'em. Some like top. Some bottom. Some both. And then it's over. Made my money. This here is a business.

I'm 23. Been out here 5 years.

I can't do this shit forever though.

# VIII

*Luther Phillips*

That boy just never can get it right. He's smart too. We all know that. His momma was smart. Simon and Jerry told me they saw him over there on Drexel. Now why they gonna tell me that? Don't no father want to know that. I don't need to know his business. He ain't gotta be out there. Shit. One day I drove over that way. And there he was. I watched him get into a car with some man. Some old fuck. Followed him over to a motel. Saw him lead the guy into a room. Made sure he didn't see me. But there he was. Boy from me. There he was.

I guess we all got to find our ways.

## IX

Sometimes I watch myself turn tricks in the mirror hanging over the dresser in my motel room. Seeing two of me. One on the bed, one protecting.

# X

The day Shelly and I moved in together I gave her 7 crisp hundred dollar bills.

Here take this.

What's this for?

Rent.

Bray, I gave the guy a check, they don't take cash. Gave him a cashiers check. Put it in your checking account for next month.

I didn't have a checking account. I worked with cash. And the little money I made over at Marshalls I cashed at the liquor store on Drexel. If this beautiful girl knew. If she knew. Shelly did things the right way. College. Job that had a future. Family fucked up but still together.

No you keep it, just put it in yours for next month.

You getting a few more hours at work Bray?

Some.

# XI

*Luther Phillips*

He blames me for his momma passing. I take it.
He just don't know.

# XII

My brother died right around the corner from Motel 99. Hit the black pavement in front of Fat Burger. This is how that went down. Some Blood shot him in the back of the head. Shot him through the mouth too. Brother wasn't even no Crip either. Shit. Just with the wrong people at the wrong time on the wrong block.

That's fucked up though.

# XIII

*Simon Murphy*

Yep. Sure did. Saw Luther's oldest son over there walking the street. Little faggot giving himself to man after man. Sad. I told Luther. Father should know what his flesh is up to. I don't wanna hear this. I told him you better listen. Your boy is out there in full force. Last time I talked to Luther? The day I told him his son was out there on Drexel.

I don't know who killed that boy.

# XIV

Shelly, I got no place to go.

# XV

Bray?

# XVI

Shelly. You look so beautiful.

Thank you Bray.

How did I end up with this fine girl? Look at her. All that brown hair. Them green eyes. She didn't run too much anymore but you could look at her and know she ran track in high school. Love how her calves rounded out so nicely then smoothing out to her thin white ankles.

You ready?

No.

Come on.

The day I met her parents gave me so much anxiety I masturbated in the bathroom between dinner and dessert. Found a nice picture of Kate Hudson in her mom's *O* magazine.

# XVII

*A poem written by Regina Pearlman seven days before she succumbed to AIDS.*

**Even Butterflies Cry**

I lost one son
To the gangs of this dirty/dusty city,
And losing another
To that savage street of Drexel.
But I understand,
These are the journeys we move through.
And I don't have much time left
So I hold my face right,
No time to lay a frown down.

The other day my boy Bray came.
I said momma is dying.
I'm going to die right here
in this bed. You hear me?
He just looked at me,
His eyes on fire,
And said no momma you ain't dying
You livin' right now.
I picked my chin up
And we both sat on my bed cryin'.

# XVIII

*John #1 with Detective Armstrong*

Oh you mean the guy who always wears that old pea coat. Wears that coat and that old beat up Cubs hat sun in or sun out. I never got with him. Too skinny. Not my type.

*Are you high?*
What?
*I said are you high?*
No. And I haven't seen him in a while.
*He's dead.*
What?
*The boy is dead.*
I wasn't one of his clients.
*Yeah? Tell you what. Turn your raggedy ass car around and make your way home. Stay the fuck off Drexel, won't you.*

# XIX

One time I had this dude who picked me up. We head back to my motel room. He takes off his brown leather belt. Hands it to me. Gets butt naked. Tells me to tie the belt around his neck. Tighter. Pull it tighter. Choke me. I pull it. Spank me. Beat my ass. So here I am my left hand controlling the belt, now a noose around this dude's neck. Tighter. My right hand slap slap slap on his ass. Harder. Harder. Dude just wanted to be choked and spanked. Soon he came. Paid me 2 hundy for that one. I didn't even have to take my clothes off.

# XX

Another time this couple hired me. Could have been husband and wife. I don't know maybe just girlfriend boyfriend. The dude takes me while his girl watches. Her eyes blank. You knew she didn't want to be there. Then he asks me to do his girl. But I said naw. I got a girl. Shelly. So dude fucked his girl all the while asking me to give him a rim job. Crazy shit. I got paid well.

# XXI

Shelly . . . don't try to save me, you can't.

# XXII

The first time I met Bray his eyes smiled at me. They were dancing. They were really dancing.

# XXIII

*Kenny with Detective Armstrong*

What did you call him? *Braydon*. Oh you mean Bray. You mean Shine. Shine, right? Yeah I saw him just the other day. Right over there standing in front of the Bluethroat.

*What's up with the name Shine?*

His eyes, man. You never seen his eyes? Like your boy Terrence Howard . . . you seen his eyes right?

*Howard, the dude in that black swim movie. Pride or some shit?*

What? I don't know. I saw him in that flick *Crash*. His eyes. He has these eyes that shine. That's how Bray's eyes are. Out here on Drex, we call him Shine.

*Well he's dead.*

What? My boy's dead?

# XXIV

*Detective Armstrong . . . searching*

**(Notes)**

Braydon Luke Phillips (AKA — Shine)

Occupation — Streetwalker with the main stomp through on the Drexel Strip. Also worked 8-16 hours a week at Marshalls Department Store (Lane Drive).

Girlfriend was Shelly Blake. Lived together. But had broken up four days before Shine was found dead.

Age — 23 — would have turned 24 the day after his murder.

Brother, Byron Keith Phillips, shot to death. May have been a Crip . . .?

Mother, Regina Pearlman, died of AIDS. Mount Cross Hospital. Contacted HIV from a boyfriend (extra marital relationship).

Father, Luther Zed Phillips, alive.

*Press on.*

# XXV

Where's momma?

She ain't here.

Let me tell you somethin' little man.

Naw I gotta go.

Boy sit your ass down before I . . .

Before you what? I gotta go.

Boy don't think you can just pop in and out of this house when you please. Come in here eat up all my food. Shit. I'm payin' the bills up in this place. You hear me? You ain't doin' shit with your life.

I got a job.

Oh ok. You gotta a job. You payin' some of the rent in here? You buyin' groceries? No you ain't. Whenever I see you, you up in my fridge. Using my hot water. Using my lights. You 18 now. You ain't goin' to school.

What you so mad about pops?

No no no. No. I'm a little more than mad. I'm pissed off.

About what?

Boy get the fuck out my house. Just get up outta here.

Tell momma I was here.

I ain't tellin' her nothin'.

# XXVI

And he was right. I didn't have a job. No money to really go to college. I didn't want to be in college anyway. My brother Byron spending more time in the streets than in school. Momma at the house less and less. I didn't want to see his grumpy/depressed ass. So I started hanging on Drexel. Fascinated by how the street worked. All the sex. Sex on my mind a lot. Hookers sliding up on cars. Sometimes getting in. Car rollin' down a dark quiet side street. I would follow sometimes. Peek from a distance. Live silent movies. Blow jobs. Quick hand jobs. Fogged windows. Back end of a car bouncing. Gay dudes selling they bodies too. Walking fast up and down Drexel. They was gettin' into cars too. Some leading dudes into motel rooms. I liked to walk past the doors. This shit was really happening. At some doors I'd hear what was up inside. You like that? Yeah? But mostly just a rhythmic bump bump bump bump bump of flesh.

Met this dude named Kenny who was a year ahead of me at Vernon. He told me this is how he makes his money. You gay?

Don't matter if I am or not. Out here. Out here on Drexel you gonna find that it don't matter. Feel me?

Naw. Well I feel you a bit but you doin' it with dudes. Right?

Right. Yeah I'm doin' it with dudes.

And you ain't gay?

Shine, check it. When you out here you makin' money. See what I'm saying? It don't matter.

# XXVII

Met Shelly when I was 21. She came in. I was working the customer service island at Marshalls.

# XXVIII

He told me one night that sometimes even when he is with me he felt lonely. Bray always seemed to be in his head. I love you Shelly. He told me that all the time. You know he could be home sitting with me and I would feel his body detaching from me. His heartbeat quickening. Kiss me on the lips and tell me I gotta get some air. Nervous Bray is what my dad called him. I never told Bray that.

*And you knew about Drexel. Right?*

# XXIX

*A poem written by Regina Pearlman the day she stepped out on her husband.*

**Well**

What's done is done — yeah
I'll walk right back in that house tonight
And let him rush into me
I know I will
But something in me is changing

I can feel my skin
I can hear the
Beat beat beat
Under my breasts

Yes, Luther,
I'm coming home to you tonight but
But
But I've met a man
Say I've met me a man

# XXX

A red Impala slows to the curb. 2 dudes. Young. Inside. Dude in the front seat on the passenger side asks me *how much*? I don't answer. He ain't serious.

Did you hear me? I said how much you selling your faggot ass for?

I hit my stride. Move along the sidewalk. Sun sinking fast. Pick up my stride. See the Impala. Red in the corner of my left eye.

How much faggot?

I ain't for sale.

What?

Keep my stride. Impala now 20 or so feet ahead of me. Stops. Driver gets out. Up on me.

Hey did you hear my friend talking to you?

Yeah, I'm done for the night. Y'all don't want me. Just lookin' to fuck with somebody. That's all you lookin' for.

You know I should beat your ass right here. You're fucking disgusting. Hope you catch AIDS out here too.

Feel two hands. Heavy. Go into my chest. Use my own two hands to catch myself on the cement. Driver back in the car. Reverse. Passenger yelling. Next time I see you out here walking around I'm going to fuck you up real bad. Wheels turning fast. The word faggot blowin' into my face.


I went home early that night.

Sat on the RTD thinking about Steen Fenrich and Matthew Shepard. These two boys killed for being gay. My momma cut out an article in the paper about

Shepard. Found an essay in a book about Fenrich. Gave both to me.

But shit, I ain't even gay.

# XXXI

Hey Bray.

Hey.

You ever think you might be bisexual?

Huh? Why you asking me that? Come on Shell. And why you laughin'? What you just asked there is a serious ass question.

It's an honest question.

Then why you laughin'?

At the way your eyes opened when you heard me ask it. They opened wide and if you would have seen your face how it became so stern.

That's a deep question. How you gonna ask your boyfriend that? No. I'm not bi.

Are you?

I don't think so. But I experimented with some girls in college. And it was nice. Flesh is flesh Bray.

# XXXII

*Kenny*

Look at my boy now. Shine you a straight up hustler now.

# XXXIII

*An hour and twenty minutes before the first bullet took Byron Keith Phillips down.*

Naw. Naw. Naw. Naw I don't know. You think she's sick? Yeah. Ok. I'll go by and see her. I'll go in the mornin'. Damn bra. Ease up. I gotta a life, you know? Hey she still over on Westchester and 10<sup>th</sup> Ave. Right? Yeah I met Harold a few times. Nope. Ain't talked to pops in a month or so. Alright bra. Love you too.

Byron?

Yeah. He thinks my momma is real sick. Damn we just saw her a couple of weeks ago. She looked alright to me. Had a little cough. Maybe lost a little weight. Did she look alright to you? Shell?

I'm glad you're going to see her.

But did she look alright to you?

I've seen her healthier.

Will you go with me tomorrow?

Sure. How's Byron?

He sounded rushed.

# XXXIV

*Luther Phillips*

I know there ain't no God now. And if there is.
Somebody tell him why. Tell that muthafucka up
there. Why you take all three from me? Ask him that.
Why you take my boys? My wife? Why you take
'em? Why'd you snatch them up? Quick like. Less
than a year and they gone. Tell them Christians at the
church on the corner they ain't no muthafuckin' God
hanging around my house.

# XXXV

*John #2 with Detective Armstrong*

*I'm not here to arrest you. Just want to ask you some questions about a young man.*

I was looking for an ATM.

*Look man; you walked up and down this street 3, 4, 5 times. I could. If I wanted. Cite you for loitering with the intent to solicit a prostitute. So you can help me out. Right? Now I saw you looking at the dudes down the street. So you ever seen him? Here take it. Look at him good. Name is Braydon. Out here they call him Shine. Now there's not a whole lot of males out here selling their bodies. So I'm guessing if you come down here often you seen him before. Right? Look man. Relax. Just give me some truth. Tell me what you know about this boy.*

I saw him at least 3 times within the last couple of months.

*So when was the last time you saw him?*

Two Saturdays ago. Went to his room. Right over there at Motel 99. I came back to see him last weekend but couldn't find him.

*Two Saturdays ago you said?*

Yeah. If something happened to him I didn't . . .

*I'm not accusing you. And like I tell all the johns down here on Drexel. Put a condom on. You can catch some deadly shit in them rooms you be up in.*

# XXXVI

Come on Bray.

Naw. This is far as I'm goin'. Sharks.

Come on.

Naw Shelly. You go. I'm cool right here.

Come ride the waves. You'll love it.

Naw. I'm good. I'll watch you. Go ahead I'll watch.

And there she went. Water to knees. Water to waist. Just her head bobbin' now waiting for a wave to bring her back. Bring her back to me. All smiles. Ponytail. My favorite. Pulled tight. Purple scrunchie.

Bray. Come on out.

Sharks. I'm good.

And here she comes. Rides a green wave back to me.

# XXXVII

*The day after Byron's funeral.*

Can you believe this? HIV.

Well at least. At least at the moment she has HIV and not AIDS.

Don't patronize me or her Shelly.

I'm not. I'm telling you just because a person has HIV doesn't always mean that the person will develop AIDS. You can live with HIV. That's all I'm saying to you Bray.

Fuck. First Byron. And now my momma. I gotta get my shit proper.

What do you need to get proper?

Stuff.

# XXXVIII

Went down to Plan Parenthood. Free HIV testing on Wednesdays. Hope I ain't got the HIV. The AIDS. Tricks use condoms.

Had a couple break off in me though over the years.

Some nights. Saying . . . Semen. Oh shit.
Condom must have broke.
No shit.

# XXXIX

Shelly. What about her? Besides the pill that's all we use. Fuck.

# XL

*Regina Pearlman*

## Harold

This young woman
Could have been me
Some years back
Tells me my immune system is failing

HIV hammering inside
And I know

Just a matter of time before AIDS is on me
Flesh opening to infection after infection

Time to rest
Let my body go

Funny thing
Harold had no idea

Semen rushing inside me
He's pushing deeper into me
Legs wrapped around his back

One body moving
We just didn't know

I'm HIV positive Harold

What?
You never had a test?
Harold had no idea

# XLI

Slow on Drexel tonight. Holidays. Folks, even the dudes lookin' to pay the women, stayin' in. Damn near XMAS. 8:30 and I'm hot in my pea coat. Weird weather in Jillings. Meetin' Shelly at 10 for a movie. Decide to give it one more stroll. Push play on my pod, glide to Terence Trent D'Arby. Somebody told me he changed his name. I like his old stuff much. Underrated. I watch my baby blue suede Pumas hit the concrete in rhythm to D'Arby's *If You Let Me Stay*. I play it again. Lookin' forward to seeing Shelly.

Shine. Shine.

Kenny.

Slow night hustler?

Yeah. I might roll on out.

Go see your girl? Don't look all surprised. I know you got a girl. Bet she don't know you out here. Right?

Right. What about you Kenny?

I tap this little honey around my block. But it's just sex. You know. Just like this shit out here. You hear about Stick?

Naw.

Come on I'll walk with you.

What's up with Stick?

Somebody beat his ass the other day. Busted my boy up bad. They got him good Shine. And you know Stick. Skinny ass had no chance whatsoever.

Where at?

In the alley behind The Drifter.

When you getin' out Shine? When you leaving this street? I know you think about it. What you 22, 23 now?

23. Don't know. Soon though. You?

I'll be here for a minute Shine. You feel me? Come on eyes' a blazin' let's hit our stroll. You know your boy Kenny is a muthafuckin' pro out here.

## XLII

Yes, I found out Bray was—out there on Drexel.
*So when did you find that out?*
Four days before he was killed.

# XLIII

I think my pops is goin' crazy Shell. Byron gone. Momma going.

How are you doing Bray? How are we doing?

## XLIV

I started telling myself that this one, this trick, would be the last one I turn. Been sayin' that for 3 weeks now. The other night a dude just wanted to cuddle. Didn't want sex. Didn't want a blow. Can we cuddle? Talk? How much to hold each other? 150. You're asking for a boyfriend experience. I can do 150. And there we were. Bathroom light on. Yellow. Curtains closed. Naked bodies locked. His head on my chest. This man. Maybe 29, 30 on my chest. His right hand gently going up and down my thighs. Close my eyes.

What Shelly say . . . flesh is flesh.

# XLV

Hey Shine. Guy in that blue car right there wants a threesome. Horny ass old man. Bank though. You up?

Naw.

We ain't gotta do—you know.

Naw Kenny. Ask Darren.

You sure?

I'm good.

You turnin' down good green, boy.

# XLVI

I started looking forward to seeing the dude who just wanted the boyfriend experience.

150. No sex. Just flesh touching flesh.

# XLVII

Every time Shelly and I have sex. About 3 times a month usually. In the back of my head I see bullets. What if I give my or already gave my girl but I'm already inside her.

Get those results back in 10 days. HIV dude at the clinic said he'd give me a call. Go on in and see him.

# XLVIII

*Detective Armstrong . . . searching*

**(Notes)**
Braydon Luke Phillips (AKA — Shine)

Found dead inside a room (his regular room) at Motel 99. Murder?

Russell Nobel (Motel 99 Manager) heard gun shot. 9:35PM.

Found alone in room. Was there a john? No gun. Just one bullet.

Girlfriend was Shelly Blake. (25)

Says Shine was the nervous type. Shelly - Graduate student (Psychology) wants to earn an MFT.

Brother, Byron Keith Phillips.

Not a Crip. Friends (a few) known Crips.

Mother, Regina Pearlman.

Boyfriend (Harold Jeans) alive. Remembers meeting "Lil Bray" a few times. Remembers him as being "scary quiet." Harold is HIV positive.

Father, Luther Zed Phillips.

Need to go visit him again.

Jeremy Roundabout (AKA- Stick)

8 days before Shine is found dead Stick beat to a pulp. Left in alley behind The Drifter. No arrests made. Police report said he remembers voices. Said he heard female and male voices. Then a rush of fists and boots. Found with a bloodied white pillow case over his head.

*This some sad shit here.*

# XLIX

Shelly and I. Sitting here in this taqueria, the one that we eat at at least 2 times a week. Shelly picking up her shrimp burrito. Me dipping salty tortilla chips one after another into a black salsa bowl. She looks so good. Her burrito is messy. All that rice. Beans. Green sauce running down her smooth chin. Taking her napkin from her lap wiping it away. Hitting her lips on the way back up. Shelly never wore much makeup. Didn't need it. Lips bare. Faint pink. Full.

Shelly, let's get out of here get out of Jillings.

Are you running from something Bray?

Naw.

Shelly wasn't from Jillings like me. She came here to study. You know I've been here all my life. I want to see the East Coast. You know? This dirty ass place. Hot. Backwards. Got all these good old boys driving these streets. Confederate flag stuck on every other truck.

I don't know Bray. I'm not even at the midpoint of completing my Psych program. I don't want to be here long term but I need to get my MFT. Plus. Well no I'm not ready to leave.

We sat in silence for the rest of our meal. Her Plus sitting heavy in my stomach.

# L

What's your name?

You can call me Shine.

I know. But your real name or it's Ok if you don't want to tell me.

He already told me his. Jason. On his fourth visit to my room we had sex. All the times before he paid me 150 and we cuddled naked. Him doin' most of the touching. Running his hands all over my body. The night we had sex he asked if he could pay me 300 for two hours of my time. He went in me. I went in him. Realized I liked it. The touch of this man. This scared me.

# LI

The last time Shelly and I had sex went like this. On my belly. A massage. Shelly is playing with my ass. Fingers. In and out. Feels good. Let her continue. Close my eyes. This is the first time. Her fingers in me like this. Her thumb in me. Two fingers. Maybe three. I don't know.

Why do I feel like something has gone wrong with us?

Does she know about Drexel? This feels good though. Four fingers. Something feels like Vaseline. Fingers in me.

Is this what you want?

I don't say a word. I do want this. Her fingers in me like this.

Hold on Bray. She leaves the bed. Comes back. I turn to look at her. She is securing a belt around her waist. Secure. At the front of the belt coming toward me a white dick. Almost real I think. 6, 7, 8 inches. She is strapped.

Is this what you want?

I can't look her in the eyes. Green eyes. Brown, straight hair down. Her breast, small, firm, erect. Belly tight. Her skin a match to the dick that is about to enter me.

I don't say it. Think it. Yes I want this.

You should get what you want Bray.

# LII

*Regina Pearlman*

## The Early Days

hmmm . . .
when little bray would climb them stairs
knee by knee
baby hands pulling him to the top
luther say
that boy is gonna fall and break somethin'

i tell him let 'em be
cause he gotta find his way up

hmmm . . .
the early days

byron telling me . . .
momma when i grow up
I want to be a football player
oh yeah . . . and why's that?
well . . . because i'm fast like Flash
the man in the red suit?
yep, Flash.

hmmm . . .
the early days

don't know why luther and i

didn't leave one another back then
then i guess having two kids
life moves on you
but then again
would have been a whole lot better
for all of us
during those early years

and i guess we both did
leave
but kept our bodies there

# LIII

The first time we saw pops put his hands on momma, Byron fired a flurry of punches at him. Broke his nose. Hammered his jaw. After that pops let Byron be.

We heard him walking around the kitchen later that night. High. Drunk. Saying crazy ass Byron. Crazy ass Byron. Over and over again. Fucker broke my nose. Fucker.

# LIV

*Detective Armstrong . . . off duty cruising down South 9$^{th}$ Street in search of a release.*

*South 9$^{th}$ Street. About two miles parallel to Drexel. Watch out for meth. Women. Sunken. Sagging. Crushed. Wrinkled. Aged. These women are losing their faces. These women are losing their bodies. These women are dying.*

*What you got? I don't do anything for less than 40.*

*These women have pimps. Some of these women have HIV. Some AIDS. Some are under 18. This is how it is done on South 9$^{th}$. Men roll along. Pull into motel lots. Wait. Flash hot lights on dirty windows. Woman opens door or waves him in. Price set. There are women on the sidewalk too. Up and down the pace goes. Men stop. Move on or pick up.*

*Drive. Park.*

*I know this. I do this.*

*I've made arrests on this street.*

*Tonight no arrests will be made by me. I will pull into a parking lot of a little motel set close to the freeway. I will release all I can inside some woman.*

*I do this often.*

*I do this because it keeps me from looking at myself.*

*Good old Detective Armstrong. Fucked liked all the rest out here.*

# LV

*Detective Armstrong . . . searching*

**(Notes)**
They found the boy like this:
In his motel (99) room.
On his back.
On the floor.
Bullet hole through the temple.
Left arm making a V with his left leg.
Right arm an L.
Eyes. Shining.
Clothes on. Jeans.
Shoes double knots.
San Francisco Giants long sleeve shirt.
Gray. Orange.
Bed made.

# LVI

And like that. Her apartment. Her lease. I depart.
Gone. Shelly say she's done. Love. But done. And
like that. No girl. No home.

Naw. This can't be my life. But it is.

Shelly?

# LVII

Bray?
Answer your phone Bray.
It's Shell.

Bray?

# LVIII

*Regina Pearlman*

## My Two Boys

You two
You ain't got to be
So damn rough and tough
You just don't
I held you both to my chest
Watched you both suckle/latch
Onto my breast
Time frozen
And now and now this
Silver bullet through butterscotch skin
Through white skull
You dead baby

And you

Your stroll I hear
Is the smoothest out there
Be careful
You my boy
You my oldest
And you givin' it away
For a price I know
But you still givin' it away.

# LIX

*Luther Phillips and Detective Armstrong*

Who?

*Detective Armstrong. I talked to you before.*

Who?

*Armstrong. Can you open the door? Just want to talk to you about your son.*

Which one you wanna talk about?

*Bray. Your oldest.*

He's dead.

*I know he is that's why I want to talk with you. Can you open the door?*

Who are you again?

*What?*

Who are you?

*Detective Armstrong. We talked a couple of weeks ago.*

What you want?

*To talk with you about your oldest son.*

I got no sons. Get.

*I'll be back.*

Get Get Get Get Get.

## LX

There is a new hustler on Drexel. Call him Ten-Speed. Rides the blocks on a Huffy. Brand new too. Young. White. I don't know him. Looks like he's 15.

# LXI

*Detective Armstrong*

When the bullet broke through Shine's temple.
On the right. And went through the left it left its mark
inside the drywall of the wall boarding room 22 and
23. Clean shot. A spray of blood must have made its
way out. Rapid. Who shot this boy? Got no gun. Just
a bullet. Gun held steady. Clean shot.

# LXII

Bray. Bray you could have stayed you know. Get your things in order. I didn't mean you had to leave right away. But you took it like that. Your pride. Stubborn.

Answer your phone.

Bray.

Answer your phone.

# LXIII

I'm not a whiner. Momma. Byron. You hear me? I'm not a whiner. But damn. You two took the wind from me when you left.

And pops. You went crazy. How much time you got left?

And Shell.

Shelly.

I never could be . . . I never knew how to be . . . I just couldn't be with you like you needed me to be . . . like I wanted to be.

And what do I have now?

Take me away Terence . . . *If I ever . . . get to heaven . . . say a prayer for my . . .*

Sang it Terence.

Lay it out.

Belt that out.

# LXIV

I went looking for him on Drexel. I wanted to see if he was safe. I found him.

And I asked him.

What are you going to do now? Tell me that Bray. Can you tell me that, can you?

## LXV

I like women.
And I like men.
They call that bisexual in the text books.
But they call you a faggot on the streets.

# LXVI

*6:30 PM . . . 3 hours and 5 minutes before the death of Shine.*

Shelly is here. We are sitting on a curb. Painted. Red. Silver drizzle coming from above. On us. Her faded brown wool coat. Her black mary janes. Blue frame glasses. Hair down. Straight. Part in the middle. Resting below the coat's collar. Her hands on her thighs. On her blue jeans. Shelly's fingernails. Each one. Bitten back. Face. Caramel freckles scattered. She sits so close to me I can taste her. I know her smell.

Drexel laid out before us. Kenny across the street talking to Stick. A meth-head stops to ask for money. Shelly hands her a dollar. Two girls. Kimberly. Mika. Standing by a pay phone. Waiting. Their pimp is parked at the Cloud Nine. Kitty-corner to us. These two started last night. Still in high school.

More drizzle. My Cubs hat on. A little white cub holding a white baseball bat. Stitched on. My pea coat keeping me warm. Hands sweaty. Shelly is here. But she is already gone. Gone from me. They all are gone.

Looking at Shelly breaks me.

Remember when you were young and you thought about all them things you wanted to do. Had no idea how or when. But you knew. You felt you could do it all. What were you going to do?

Lots. But here I am. Walking these streets. I'm better than this. You know?

Lots, hey Bray?

Lots. Like. I feel Shelly slipping away more now.

Her body inching away from me on this curb.

Yeah lots. But hey growing up was just some shitty days beside some good ones. The good ones though were good. I remember those big trucks stacked with hay passing our car. Momma and pops looking back at me and Byron, telling us hey boys look, hay truck passing. And all four of us would lick our right thumb place it in our left palm and make a wish.

Then the shitty ones. Too many days when . . . naw, it's alright.

You know I can't be with you, with you out here doing this . . . you know . . .

Save it. I know that.

So what are you going to do, Bray?

Think of the good times. Keep them up in me. Keep moving. Keep wishing.

# LXVII

And then I left. Left Bray on that curb. His head resting in his hands. Rain harder. I looked back twice. There he sat.

My dad always told me I picked a weak man. I never believed him. Bray was never weak. Insecure about his body. His masculinity. Yes. But not weak.

# LXVIII

*Jason*

Shine! Shine . . . Shine . . . Shine?
Oh. Oh shit.

# LXIX

*6:58 PM . . . 2 hours and 37 minutes before the death of Shine.*

I need to get up. T. Trent. Raise volume. Sing to me boy.

Hit my soul.

Meet Jason at 9.

Hit my soul.

# LXX

*Poem found in the right inside pocket of Shine's Pea Coat. Written on yellow binder paper. Written at the top. Keep this one. From your momma.*

**These Days**

Not one
Loop to jump back through

These days fading
I have nothing to go back and bend right

These days
Watching my body leave

You coming down here everyday
To say to your momma
*You got this beat*

No
I don't

You don't beat this one
Just try to stay alert

As long as you can
To watch it take parts of you

Hoping them good parts
Heart and eyes hold out the longest

# LXXI

*Kenny*
*7:39 PM . . . 1 hour and 56 minutes before the death of Shine.*

Saw him that night. Sitting in front of the motel door. Back up against the door. His little Cubs hat pulled down over his eyes.

Shine. Shine what's up? Shine. You there?

Hands deep in the pockets of his pea coat. Jeans creased. Right foot lightly bouncing off the concrete. Headphones on.

Your shit is loud.

He looked up at me. Raised his hat a bit.

You alright?

Naw. This is it Kenny. Got this one at 9. That's it. Done.

Yeah?

Done.

Alright then. Just like that.

You done?

I don't know Shine, this shit here is here.

# LXXII

Not sure what to do with his stuff. He didn't have a lot of things. A duffel bag of clothes. Some CDs. A photo album. A book of poetry his mother gave him by Sonia Sanchez.

Still hear him telling me, Shell I got a lot of issues. Just so you know. I'd say, we all do. We all do, Bray. Then he would reach for me. Kiss my neck. Tingles.

# LXXIII

*9:00 PM . . . 35 minutes before the death of*
*Shine.*

Shell . . . Shell . . . where did they go? Shell . . .
where did you go?

# LXXIV

*Regina Pearlman*

## I Wave Goodbye

when i die
when i die
when i die

throw your coat over me
that beautiful pea coat that flaps
blue wings carrying you along drexel

when i die
go check on your daddy
tell 'em to release the anger choking his heart

when i die
go see about byron
and lay down yellow and peach roses
across his grave

when i die
when i die
when i die

# LXXV

*Detective Armstrong*

*9:35 PM . . . Bullet races into the temple of Shine.*

*Gone.*

# LXXVI

*Jason tells all to Detective Armstrong. Nine days after the body of Shine is found.*

*Where do you want to begin?*
I'll just say it all.
*And we're talking about the same boy. Braydon Luke Phillips. AKA, Shine. Right?*
I knew him as Shine.
*Alright. It's on you.*

*Taking this man in. Honest. Nervous. Rocking in the metal chair. Fingers drumming the table between us. Gray polo shirt. Auburn hair neat. Eyes soft, green. And he says he was there. In that room with Shine. Says he wants to clear his conscience. So he is here.*

I met Shine on several occasions. We held each other in the beginning. He'd tell me about his girlfriend. How he wished he could be solely with her. Leave all the things he did on Drexel behind him. He would talk about his family. But not much. And sometimes we wouldn't talk at all. He would turn on his iPod, put the ear phones on and let me take his body.

The night he died. That night I met him at 9. I was a little late. Parked my car on the street, as I always did.

*On the street? Why not park by the room?*

Fear of the police following me into the parking lot. I'd park on the street a little ways down from the motel and just walk to the room. I thought I wouldn't look so obvious. So, that night we met. I walked in. Put my money on top of the TV. Shine grabbed it. Slid it into one of the inside pockets of his coat. The last time we had met, we. Well me. I wanted him to hit me as we had sex. I, I, I wanted him to punch me. Slap me.

*Did he?*

Yeah. All this anger came from him and onto me. And it felt good. His fist in my chest. Open hand slaps to the top of my head. Fists, slaps all over my body. But on that night. That night. I, I, I well. It went bad. I have a gun. Loaded. It's registered.

*Wait wait wait wait . . . what kind of work you do? Carrying a gun on you.*

You didn't run my info. yet?

*Mmmm . . . muthafucka. You a cop?*

Sheriff. A couple of hours away. In Chanzi County.

*Muthafucka. Go on, man.*

That night I brought it. I wanted something more intense. Thought we could use the gun. Thought he could use it on me. Put it to my head. Pretend to rape me. Thought. I, I, I just thought. But. And. Well.

This is how it went — I show him the gun. He takes off his coat. You want me to do what? I tell him. He takes the gun. Everything slows. He sits on the end of the bed. Turns up his iPod. I can hear the music. Look's at me. You really want me to do that? Slow motion. His right hand gripping my gun. I see him clearly. He's looking above me. His eyes. Somewhere else. Head tilted. Chin up. The song on his iPod. I hear it. Something about . . . *If I ever get to heaven* or something like that . . . *say a prayer for my mother, say a prayer for my father, say a prayer for my brother* . . . and then something like . . . *please say a prayer for me.*

And then. Slow. Gun at his temple. The sound of muffled thunder. Blood. Mini waterfalls racing down his face. Onto his shirt. Blood. He hits the floor. All so slow. I grab the gun. My body shaking.

There is a window in the bathroom. Pulling myself out. Stepping down in the alley behind the motel. I walk the alley. Make my way to the street. To my car. Shaking.

# LXXVII

I use to hear Bray in my dreams asking me how this life got so complicated. Then sometimes he would sit at my feet, Indian style, eyes closed, and say Shell, it's not so bad where I am.

But he doesn't come anymore.

# LXXVIII

*Detective Armstrong*

    *Seven days after Shine's death — his father, Luther Phillips, collapsed in his bedroom from a heart attack. He died en route to the hospital.*
    *And like that — a family gone.*

# LXXIX

*Kenny*

There was a youngster once. About three years ago.

He'd walked this street tough.

A swagger about him. Until the end. When he got tired.

Watched his family disappear.

His girl disappear.

Where's he at now?

Tell you, my boy, Shine is gone.

He moved on. He's free. Come on . . . let's hit our stroll.

## ACKNOWLEDGEMENTS

Nia and Wil, who inspire me every day to open my heart to love. Leslie Moore, our *somewhere beautiful* is here. Charles Rice-González, my brother in prose. Bhanu Kapil, Patrick Rosal, Beatrix Gates, Seven, Colleen Mills, Theresa Senato Edwards, Jonathan Brennan, Don Weise, Matthew Quick, Paul Selig, Peggy Messerschmidt, Tim Rayworth, Bruce Guernsey, Douglas Martin, Wendy Mazuelos, Natalia Menedez, Edward L. Gills, Chris Abani, Theresa Tran, and Kenny Fries.

And a heart-felt thanks to Bryan Borland, who believes in *Shine*.

## ABOUT THE AUTHOR

Donnelle McGee is a Jimi Hendrix freak and wishes he could dunk a basketball. He earned his MFA from Goddard College. He is a faculty member at Mission College in Santa Clara, California. His work has appeared in *Controlled Burn*, *Colere*, *Haight Ashbury Literary Journal*, *Home Planet News*, *Iodine Poetry Journal*, *Permafrost*, *River Oak Review*, *The Spoon River Poetry Review*, and *Willard & Maple*, among others. His work has also been nominated for a Pushcart Prize. Donnelle lives in both Sacramento and Turlock, California.

## ABOUT THE PUBLISHER

The mission of Sibling Rivalry Press is to develop, publish, and promote outlaw artistic talent—those projects which inspire people to read, challenge, and ponder the complexities of life in dark rooms, under blankets by cell-phone illumination, in the backseats of cars, and on spring-day park benches next to people studying Ginsberg and Kerouac. We believe in literary rock stars.